TWINS MAC & MADI PLAY FIELD HOCKEY

By Linda Herron

Illustrated By Marie Delon

Twins Mac & Madi Play Field Hockey

This is a work of fiction. Names, characters, places, and incidents either are the product of the author's imagination or are used fictitiously. Any resemblance to actual persons, living or dead, events, or locales is entirely coincidental.

First edition July 2024
Book design by Project 100
Book cover design by Marie Delon

ISBN 978-1-959140-13-9 (paperback)

www.BigLittlePress.com

Publisher's Cataloging-in-Publication

(Provided by Cassidy Cataloguing Services, Inc.)

Names: Herron, Linda, author. | Delon, Marie, illustrator.

Title: Twins Mac & Madi play field hockey / Linda Herron ; illustrations by Marie Delon.

Other titles: Twins Mac and Madi play field hockey

Description: First edition. | [San Jose, California] : Big Little Press, [2024] | Series: Twins Mac & Madi | Audience: Juvenile. | Summary: Twins Mac & Madi are the youngest players on their team, and they're always ready to give their best! But sometimes, the game just doesn't go their way. With the help of their wise coach, the twins learn that success isn't just about the score … it's about playing your best and always supporting your team through thick and thin!--Publisher.

Identifiers: ISBN: 978-1-959140-13-9 (paperback) | 978-1-959140-14-6 (hardcover) | 978-1-959140-07-8 (ebook)

Subjects: LCSH: Twins--Juvenile fiction. | Sisters--Juvenile fiction. | Field hockey--Juvenile fiction. | Teamwork (Sports)--Juvenile fiction. | Sportsmanship--Juvenile fiction. | Success--Juvenile fiction. | CYAC: Twins--Fiction. | Sisters--Fiction. | Field hockey--Fiction. | Teamwork (Sports)--Fiction. | Sportsmanship--Fiction. | Success--Fiction. | LCGFT: Stories in rhyme.

Classification: LCC: PZ7.1.H49465 Twf 2024 | DDC: [E]--dc23

DEDICATION

To all the incredible girls who step onto the field, court, track, or into the gym, this dedication is for you. Your determination, resilience, and passion for sports are inspiring. You show that strength is not just about physical prowess but also about the spirit, commitment, and camaraderie you bring to your team.

Sportsmanship goes beyond winning and losing; it is about respect, integrity, and the love of the game. You exemplify these values every time you play, showing grace in victory and dignity in defeat. Your sportsmanship fosters a positive environment where all athletes can thrive and grow.

To the coaches, mentors, families, and friends who support these young athletes, your encouragement and guidance are invaluable. Together, you help build not only better athletes but also better people.

Let this dedication be a reminder of the importance of inclusivity and equal opportunity in sports. May every girl feel empowered to pursue her athletic dreams and continue to champion the values of good sportsmanship.

Keep inspiring. Keep striving. Keep playing.

Linda Herron
xoxo

In the City of Warwick, where the grass is green
Live the Lady Bugs, a team of field hockey queens.

Twins Mac and Madi are the youngest of the lot.
Their skills are sharp, and they shoot a good shot.

The twins practice each day in a field down the street.
Where they learn to be smart and quick on their feet.

They dribble and pass. They shoot, and sometimes miss.
But their spirits stay strong throughout all of this.

In every single game, Mac and Madi sure try.
But there are times when even their efforts go awry.

They sometimes get frustrated and begin to feel down.
Which makes their happy smiles turn into a frown.

But their wonderful coach, so wise and so sure,
Says, "Girls, success isn't just about the score."

"It's in how you play, with grace and with cheer,
Even when a victory may not be near."

Mac and Madi listen, and they soon come to learn,
That despite any setback—any small twist or turn,

That good sportsmanship and hard work are the key,
To being a good player—win or lose, you see.

So they root for their teammates, so loud and so clear,
They encourage each player with a big, hearty cheer.

Sometimes their team wins, and sometimes they lose.
But they always have fun, with no frowns and no boos.

And soon the last game of the season will be here.

They're playing the Fireflies, a team that they fear.

The Fireflies have won every single game.
And all throughout Warwick, everyone knows their name.

But when the game begins, Mac and Madi become aware,
That the Fireflies certainly don't seem to play fair.

They push and they shove, and argue with the referee,
And they break rules when the ref can't see.

But the Lady Bugs work hard and show their team pride.
And with two minutes to go, the score remains tied.

The coach calls time out, and says, "Let's stay focused and smart. Remember what we practiced and show them your heart."

21

Soon Mac gets the ball and is about to score the winning goal,
When a Firefly trips her from behind, the crowd gasps as a whole.

The ref doesn't catch it, and Mac starts to complain,
Madi lends a hand, saying, "You know the game."

"Let's finish with honor," Madi says with a smile.
"Just the same as we've been doing all the while."

And with seconds to go, right before the whistle blows,
Madi passes Mac the ball, and in the net, it goes!

The crowds erupt in cheers, the Lady Bugs hug in a pile.
"You did it, girls!" their coach shouts with a smile.

The win feels amazing—just like a dream.
But what Mac and Madi love most is being part of a team.

And playing the game they love so dear,
With good sportsmanship and hard work, year after year.

So remember, no matter what sport you play
In field hockey or any game, come what may.

It's not just about winning, but also how you play,
With kindness, respect, and joy every day.

THE END

Author Linda Herron

Linda is a children's author, proud Rhode Islander, and identical twin who loves to craft heartwarming tales about the magic bond between siblings. With first-hand experience of the joys and struggles that being an identical twin entails, Linda was inspired to write a series of fun children's stories to help kids embrace their differences and cherish their special relationships with their sister or brother.

As a seasoned financial expert by day, when Linda isn't dreaming up new children's stories to delight and entertain her readers, she's writing business articles and blogs. Her financial expertise has been featured on major media outlets including American Express, LendingTree, and Daily Business News. Currently, Linda enjoys the sunny weather in California, but she often returns to Rhode Island to spend time with her beloved family. For more information about Linda and her books, visit her website at www.lherron.com.

Linda Herron

Illustrator Marie Delon

Marie is a Mexican illustrator based in the city of Hermosillo, Mexico. Her work is characterized by its digital techniques and mixed media, which she employs in her illustrations for independent publications and zines, children's books, and advertising - both national and international. As a full-time graphic designer, Marie also implements her illustrations into her daily job. Recently, she has been working on personal creative projects that include character design, merchandising design, and concept art for videogames. In her spare time, Marie loves watching movies, reading comic books, and playing tabletop RPG games.

www.ingramcontent.com/pod-product-compliance
Lightning Source LLC
Chambersburg PA
CBRC090843120626
46551CB00009B/747